THE WISEMAN

THE LIES BEHIND THE TRUTH

RISHI GARG

Contents

Prologue

Always lived with an introverted family, Dentom was scared of talking to an extroverted society. Although he was not an extrovert but always tried to build his confidence. He was a good one in his studies which helped him in becoming a lawyer. Being always bullied because of his introverted behavior, he always remained depressed. Although this story is fictional but it will take you to a non-fictional world where I have shown the different types of sorrow, grief, chaos, difficulties, and obstacles to surviving in this selfish society. You can read it and if you are a person who loves to be challenging always, You can sense and feel it! Folks Congrats to be a part of the separate community.

1

THE MISERY OF THE NEW YORK

Near the pleasant city of New York, there was an advocate who lived there. His all-time aim was to be on the path of truth. As he had taken an oath that he never will say a lie, he always said the truth. His name was Dentom Texas . As he was a truth-teller and an advocate, therefore he was not able to win such cases as other smart advocates who always use dirty tricks and lies to win cases. Sometimes, he thank why he had chosen the job of an advocate. As he was not winning the cases, he got depressed. His depression and case loss news was such famous among the people of New York that they even call him as the Misery of the New York. One day he decided to leave his profession. When he was going to resign from the administrative office of lawyers. Suddenly, an old woman came to her. The woman was looking in a miserable condition and dissatisfied with herself. Dentom frequently asked if she wanted money or any other thing. The woman started crying. Denton got emotional. He asked the woman what was her name. The woman replied that her name was Mandrid. As the Dentom was an advocate, he had a very great sixth sense. He frequently sensed that might be the woman needed help. Therefore he asked the woman if she needed any help from himself. As the woman was shivering with the winter, he took the woman along with him to his home. That incident, that lady might be indirectly saved his profession and his career. Later, the woman told him that he had to file a case against God. Listening to that Dentom laughed and he requested her to please tell him about her real problem. The woman cried at him and said that she was not lying. Dentom kept close his mouth as he got scared after seeing an angry version of the Mandrid. Mandrid told that her son and daughter in law were killed. Killers had taken his grandson along with them. Dentom was not seeming interested in her story as he was not concentrating on her story. Suddenly Mandrid bought fainted. Dentom got worried. He frequently ran to the city hospital along with Mandrid. When he reached the hospital there was a long line. Dentom took place in line as he thank that the line will segregate in a few minutes. All got wrong as he was thinking. After standing for almost 2 hrs in the line. He got frustrated. When he came close to the reception, he came to know that he had not carried his wallet along with him. All attention, time and hard work went in vain. It was a situation like in a cricket match a fielder is running from the offside of the field to the leg side of the field to save the boundary, he puts his dive but his dive all goes in vain. As he didn't had the money, he came out of the long queue. After that, he decided to see Mandrid once before going the home. When he reached the bench where he left the Mandrid. He got more tensed and frustrated as Mandrid was missing. He frequently started to search for her. He asked all the staff and doctors about Mandrid but all had the same reply that they hadn't seen her. After a search or hunt of 3 hours for Mandrid. Dentom lost his cool, he decided to forget the Mandrid and reached back his house after a drive of 1 hr as there was heavy traffic which nearly had taken the test of his patience. When he was parking his car in his Garage, the bumper of the car got collided with his Motorcycle. Those incidents might be forced him to thank that all mishaps were happening only to him. When he came out of the car and saw the dent in the car. He lost his cool and kicked his car with a toe kick. His car got a new memory and he fractured his foot. He started crying. As he was living in a very deserted place. He didn't had any neighbour. His house was in a forest as he loved to live near nature but one thing that was close to his house was a graveyard. Then it was the time of evening came, all around outside the house was dark. As Denton's foot got fractured, he decided to went to the hospital again but that time, he was not in a state of standing in a queue. So he decided to went his friend's clinic which was not a big one but as we know that in times of trouble, even a donkey has to make father. He started his Splash. Ridding with a fractured foot was not an ordinary task but he was a man of his aim and his words. It was a thrilling ride for him. After coming from the hospital, he even didn't get a chance to enter his house. All the series of events that happened with him that day was a real patience test for him. And unfortunately, he lost his test on the last point. After a dreadful and painful journey. Dentom reached his friend's house. He parked his bike outside the house as his friend was not a rich one who had a garage like him. He entered his friend's house whose name was Vibrad Ve Olivia. As he went inside the house, he saw the dead body of his friend. Vibrad was lying on the floor near the couch. With a fractured foot, a person who was suffering from the morning a, who had seen his friend's corpse in front of him who was his only relative, how could he had more hope left in him of living. The same happened with him. Dentom left all his hope. He went to the kitchen and brought a knife along with him. Then the emotions took place of patience. He cried with a Loud and impactful scream, " Why God, why God, why I am the only one who suffered more than anyone. I'm such a kind person who never told a lie in his entire life, who never did a wrong deed with anyone, always did helping deeds, never think about myself, Why every time only I suffered, why all my life went in vain "? He took the knife and slashed down his own throat and got died. That scream, that day hurt the God most! Might be that day that God had ended the Misery of New York also!

2

THE EXPEDITION OF DREAD AND DELIGHT

The Misery of New York has been abolished but indirectly by God. Dentom had died and his soul was not ready to leave his body easily. God of Death arrived. God said "Hey now it is the time to left the body ". Dentom 's soul disagreed with the proposal straight away. Listening to the reply, God of Death got enraged and was ready to curse him suddenly God of Justice came there. Then, he stopped the God of Death to curse him. As the god of Death was enraged and dissatisfied with the spirit's reply, he frequently asked him " why I left him, why I don't curse him. He had stopped me, the God of Death to do my deed "? Listening to his question, God of Justice started laughing. Seeing him, God of Death got more enraged and dissatisfied. He cried that Answer my question first. Seeing them both with different thoughts, opposing each other, Dentom0 soul went in perplexity. With a pleasant and a modulated voice, God of Justice answered that the dentom's soul had experienced a lot of difficulties while living his life and the main point was that he experienced difficulties or troubles even though he had never said a lie, never irritate anyone, never thank bad about anyone and never did a wrong deed in his life. After listening to the answer, the anger of God Of Death got segregated. He asked God of Justice for a few minutes. God of Justice approved that proposal. Might be they wanted to discuss how will they bring the soul with them in that period. With a warm voice, God of Justice again asked the soul if It will come or not. That time, soul approved his proposal. Might be the soul had a trust in God of Justice that God of Justice will surely justify her case. Then the journey to Heaven started. When they all were going to Heaven, suddenly, God of Death told them that he can't go there. Soul again went in perplexity. Soul asked God of Justice " Why the God of Death can't go to heaven". Listening to his question, God of Justice answered him that God of Death was the God in Hell. He cannot go to heaven as he had not been permitted to go to Heaven. His range was only limited to Hell. As the three had to leave the God of Death in Hell. As they were going Hell first, in the path the soul saw the blazing, fiery flames of fire. Seeing that horrible path, soul got scared. God of Justice relaxed him and said that those flames will not harm the soul until their case will be discussed in the Court of Gods. Listening to that answer, the soul got more tensed and scared as it was thinking that if it will be declared an evil spirit in the Court of Gods , he will have to face those blazing flames and many more horrible things in Hell. As they were going forward in their path , they saw a big cauldron which was full of the oil which was Kept on the burning fire. Seeing that was not looking so horrible but when the soul saw that the evil spirits were fried in that cauldron as their punishment. Seeing that scene , God of Justice started laughing . As the soul's most of the mind was already frightened by the flaming fires and by that frying of evil spirits in the cauldron earlier. And after listening to that sweet but horrible laughing of God of Justice, the soul got fainted. Might be the soul was not able to handle that pressure or that fear which was not cast on it. Everywhere was blood flowing and monsters were roaring at that moment with a dreadful voice. After a horrifying time for soul, they reached hell . At the Gate of Hell, there was a dragon standing who was looking in anger. His name was Zugh. God of Justice left the group of the three and went into his palace. Then the pleasant, loving, sweet ride started. As the left two were going into Heaven, the fairies and mermaid were standing and dancing at the corners of the path. Suddenly, the soul woke up. Seeing that beautiful scenes, Soul got amazed and very glad. Then it's all fear was might be lost in a few minutes. It was enjoyable at that moment. God of Justice was also looking happy that time as he saw the happy side of the soul first time since he met him. The path to heaven was a treat to feel and watch. All around were the light blue clouds that can make a person happy from sad, pleasant sounds and songs were playing at that time there was playing by the God of Music. After a delightful journey, the soul and God of Justice reached the Gate of Heaven. At that door, a fairy whose name was Vimin came and welcomed them with a beautiful garland and a sweet song. Then the Expedition of dread and delight ends!

3

THE BIRTH OF THE WISEMAN

God of Justice entered with the soul in the Heaven. Seeing that beautiful scene, soul started dancing. Suddenly a group of Satyrs came and ordered the soul to be straight. Soul got scared of them by their loud voice. They made the soul their hostage and God of Justice started laughing very loudly. Suddenly a thunder came and the God of Justice changed his appearance. Then, the God of Justice became the God of Mischief. Seeing that horrible change, the trust of soul got decimated as he was thinking that a bad joke has happened to him. He got in perplexity that why that bad joke has happened to him. He wanted the same question's answer from Satyrs but they told him that His question will be revealed soon. Soul's world was revolving around that moment for him . It got fainted again. When the spirit woke up, it saw itself in a chamber with no windows, only with a spirit who was looking depressed with itself. Seeing another spirit, the Texas spirit got some relaxation. It started to interact with another spirit. First It asked his name. Then another spirit replied that its name was Euri.

Listening to its name, the Texas spirit started to laugh at it very loudly. The Euri's spirit got more depressed. Then the Texas spirit asked Euri spirit How had he come here in this vulnerable chamber. Listening to that question, Euri 's eyes got filled with blood. Suddenly he came into a wave of disastrous anger. He assembles his all left power and choked the Texas spirit's throat with his powerful hands. Doing that horrible actions, Euri suddenly started crying. He told Texas that he had the power to watch the past as he was living in that chamber for the past 10000 years. While he was sobbing in tears, he said that something was wrong happened with him. He will surely take his revenge. When he was to start his story suddenly a Satyr came and take the Texas soul along with him. He unlocked the gate of the chamber and called the spirit of Texas out. The Satyr tied a black piece of cloth on the eyes of Texas. When that black rag opened, the spirit saw himself as standing in a circle with handcuffs in his hands around the Multiple Gods such as God of Truth, God of anger and many more in the Court of Gods. Suddenly a big announcement was made, the God of Justice arrived on his royal elephant whose name was Seron. Seeing the Real God of Justice, the spirit became angered. Soon the God of Justice sat on his throne and ordered to start the case. The Court was the same as the Court on Earth. The Texas spirit was feeling odd, a little ashamed and very awkward as he was a lawyer who fought cases to save the innocent when he lived on Earth but in heaven he was the one who has standing in the witness box on whom the case was discussing. Thinking and thinking, he realised that one on earth has a choice in his hands whether he wants to be discussed in the Court or not but In the Gods Court, one has no choice, everyone had to stand there occasionally once after his life. After the prestigious announcement, the case started. The Heaven lawyers started by saying that Texas spirit hadn't done any wrong deed in his life, he spent his life with difficulties and died a dreadful death. The God of Justice understood all the cases only with a few statements from heaven lawyers The God of Justice was ready to declare his judgement suddenly the spirit asked the Gods if they will answer his question or not. God of Justice understood his question before he said anything. Might be the God of Justice can read anyone's mind if he wanted. The God of Justice answered the same as Satyr answered earlier that His question will be revealed soon. That answer made the spirit more upset. The God of Justice declared that the spirit will be awarded a new life again as an advocate for his good deeds and crystal clear truths in his life as Dentom Texas. Then, the God of Justice cleared that the spirit will take birth in the name of Emos McQueen and after taking birth as Emos McQueen will choose the profession of a lawyer again but this time, the spirit will become a very intelligent and a mastermind person. He ended his judgement by saying that the spirit will never forget his past of being Texas even after taking birth as Emos McQueen. After listening to that judgement, the series of questions started erupting in the mind of the spirit. Again the God of Justice understood his question before the spirit said something. God of Justice again answered with the same answer that Your Questions will be revealed soon. Till then three questions were collected into the mind of the spirit but unfortunately, he had no answer. He became more upset and started thinking that in the human court, at least the questions are revealed but there in the court of God, every question has the same answer " Your Question will be revealed soon ". Suddenly, after the judgement, the God of power asked if they will give some powers to spirit or not. God of Justice laughed and said that his intelligence and his mastermind will be his powers and he clarified more by saying that, When the spirit will take birth as Emos, he will have three more powers which are hidden and when the powers will be needed to him, he will be automatically realised his power. The God Of Justice ended his judgement by saying that the spirit had awarded one more life to diminish all the cases which were left pending in court on Earth planet or the cases in which, the malpractices were used to win the cases. In last, he said that when the spirit in the look of Emos McQueen will win the cases for the poor or the people who had been broken from inside and had left their will to get justice, the Emos will be called or known as WISEMAN by the public on earth. That big judgement closes the case of the spirit of Texas, the court adjourned and the spirit thanked all gods for their alms deed. The God of Justice replied that they hadn't done any alms deed on him, he have to pay for this soon. Listening to the word soon from the God of Justice's mouth, again and again, maxed the spirit annoyed and irritated. Might be the word soon became the most irritating word for the spirit. That Golden Judgement and that silver hearing in court resulted in the BIRTH OF THE WISEMAN!

4

EMOS MCQUEEN: THE TRUE HOMECOMING

On a dusky, swarthy and nebulous night, the mightiest born. He was born in a family that lived in the countryside of Buckinghamshire. Their earnings came from a farm on which they have 23 horses, 50 cattle and 25 goats. His family believed in Christianity. As the God of Justice said earlier his family named him Emos McQueen When he was only 7 months old he said his first words. That golden words were “ Paa ” to his dad. As he was God gifted child to his family. Now the question will be arises in your mind will be “ why did only that McQueen family get that God gifted special child. the McQueen family did several fasts to remove a curse on them that was they will never see a boy child face in their family till they didn’t make the God happy The curse was given by a Buddha priest because of their bad deeds. The McQueen family didn’t See a boy child in their family in their last 3 generations. Each generation tried their best to make happy the god. But unfortunately, all went in vain. But when Emos took birth, their curse got removed as it meant that they made God happy by their hard work and their worship. That reason also makes the child special to them. Days passed, and the season changed. Emos got three years old. At that small, he learned to walk, dance and speak fluently. One day, a mysterious fire broke out on his farm in the evening. As his all family members were gone out somewhere, he was alone in his house with her mother. Frequently when the mother came to know about the fire, she ran to save the cattle and their other pets. And then the most dreadful moment came in Emos's life as he saw her mother burning in the fire in front of him despite saving their pets. Seeing his mom burning, baby emos could not control his emotions and decided to save his mother from that fire. When he jumped into that fire, a flame of fire caught him. To save his loving one, the true friend of emos came heroically. It was a horse. His name was Quer. Putting his all efforts to save the emos, fortunately, he became successful in saving him. Quer took the baby emos along with him by placing Emos on his back. It was such a miracle that an animal saved the life of a human. It showed the great affection and the love between them. After some 3 hours, emos found himself in a waterfall that was situated in the middle of the forest. Being a small child, he got worried and scared after seeing himself in a forest alone. His tension was already high but when he saw a big burn on his back, it makes him tenser and his tension went to the next level. When he noticed that Quer was missing, he started finding him but none other than failure, he found with his attempt. He was only a 3 years boy, after some time he started feeling hungry. He left his attempt to find the Quer and started a new research to find the food in the forest. After deep research of 5 hours, unfortunately, he found nothing. The time passed but no solution came to the mind of emos. When he founded nothing to eat, he got fainted. When he woke up the next day, he found himself in a box. He got suffocated and started knocking the box from inside. He screams for help but no one listened to his scream. Again he had no choice and he was feeling tired with no energy. He got fainted in that box. His situation became like a half-dead body. As he had the blessings of God, he survived in that miserable condition also. The box in which the emos were present, was the box of the Vikings tribes of that Forest in which they kept the humans which were used for their meal. Soon after the emos got fainted again, the beats of the drum started playing. The Annual party of Vikings started. They were preparing very different cuisines and for the test, the people were dancing in between them to the drum beats. All over there was a fest. The king of Vikings was to arrive suddenly they noticed the sound of firing bullets in the air. That sound made them very worried and scared. All started to run here and there and it created a great mess among them. After firing nearly 25 bullets, a man came with a walrus moustache, a turban on his head and in a forest officer dress. He fired a bullet at the king and the king died. When the king dies, all Vikings went frightened. The man ordered them to be in a straight line. He arranged the Vikings according to their height. Then, he ordered them to sit in his truck which was parked some 500 metres away. The public had no choice except to follow the order as the man spread out his superiority among them by killing their king. Unexpectedly when they all were leaving that place, the man saw the wooden box in which Emos was kept. He thanks that might be the box will be filled with treasure or consist of some valuable assets of the Vikings. He called two people to lift the box aand place it into the truck. Two healthy men came and placed that box in their giant car. When all were ready to leave the forest suddenly a person cried that plz someone tell him where were they going? The Officer shot the man and said that they were going to Hell in anger. They were coming to the dockyard of the Buckinghamshire from the Countryside. Then the Journey to the Dockyard started. The caravan which started from the forest then reached the dockyard. Now the question arises, why, why dockyard? Stay with us, it will be revealed soon. A person came and informed us that the bidders were eagerly waiting for the merchandise. That statement from the person showed clearly that cruelty was on the par level with the officer. He was considering the people as the merchandise, after all, he was a criminal as he did the worst crime of human trafficking on the earth. When all Vikings were leaving the truck, the officer commanded one of the Vikings to bring the box along with him. When the commanded person was bringing the box suddenly he dropped the box and the truth opened. All got shocked except that commanded Viking as he had already known that the box had a child in it. The evil mind of the officer frequently started to make use of children. The officer took him in his hands and brought him to his room. As he didn't know the name of the child and he fainted. First, he tried to wake the child and when he got success in it, secondly he gave some food and water to him. Emos ate something after 2 days. Then the officer started his enquiry to know the name of the child. In a light voice, he asked the child what was his name. The child didn't respond to him. It made the officer angry. Then he understands that might be the child's mind was got whitewashed when he was dropped by the

Vikings. When the child was eating the biscuits suddenly the officer noticed a locket on his neck. When he opened it, he saw that the child's name was written on it which was EMOS. The officer got amazed. He ordered a cradle for him and ordered his servant to take care of the child especially. Then, the criminal went for the crime. The auction ended in almost 5 hours. That human trafficking earned a lot of money for him. Then, he again went to meet EMOS. After the auction, he started thinking that how he could be made the child productive for him. A lightning idea came to his mind to sell the baby EMOS. Might be it was a cruel idea but in another manner, it could be a wise idea also as the baby will get new parents and be better taken care of when he will be sold out. The officer did the same in his planning. Might be it was a god's blessing, he found a couple who didn't have a child in only 2 days. Then the coincidence of the century happened, where the name of the real family of emos was McQueen, and the name of the family which bought him from the officer was also McQueen. Officer sold emos for such a pile amount that was 2 million dollars to the McQueen family. Officer told them that the name of the baby was emos and if they wanted they could change his name. The family loved the name Emos when they listened to it the first time. They replied that they were very happier with the name emos as it was seeming different in listening than others. The family took the baby from the officer and brought him along with them to their luxurious villa in Buckinghamshire. From a farm, now the emos was living in a Villa. That marketing between the couple and the officer marked the true homecoming of Emos McQueen. As everything that happens on earth has a reason behind it, therefore surely that homecoming of emos also had a reason behind it.

5

THE FIRST GLIMPSE OF DEEP OBSERVANCE

Two were shot and one was hiding. The shooter warned him to come out but hiding one didn't pay any heed to the shooter. All there was dark and the cacophony was making the atmosphere very unpleasant. Suddenly the cell phone of the hiding one rang. Shooter noticed it frequently by his sharp sense. He walked down only three steps and professionally shot the hiding one. Then he laughed in a sweet voice and said " I am the devil of my words ". As the shooter completed his dialogue, the rounds of applause took the place of cacophony and lights opened. The organiser announced that the role of the shooter was played by our one and only beloved Emos McQueen and the role of casualties were played by our loving Word, Sam and Fam. The audience clapped for all of them but one thing which was not accepted by the Word was that the audience was chanting only emos ' s name. It created a feeling of partiality and financial discrimination as the emos were a child of a royal family and the fam, and Sam and word are the children of the family which were not as rich as the emos family. That play sowed the seeds of the Greatest betrayal of Buckinghamshire which was yet to come. After that play, the hatred for emos in word heart was at a par level. In last, the organiser announced to the audience " Play is finished, now you all can go ". At that time, Our protagonist, Emos was only 5 years old and at that little age, our hero spoke English very fluently. His language was so pure, cognate, classical and impactful as the language of an advocate. And why not? After all, the prediction was already made by the God of Justice about Emos very earlier. One of the servants of the McQueen family came, picked up Emos and dropped him at the McQueen Mansion. The servant went for another work. Mrs . McQueen was already waiting eagerly for Emos and her name was also Mandrid McQueen . What was that coincidence as the name of the woman who met with the Dentom Texas in the administrative office of lawyers was also Mandrid ? It will be revealed soon but one thing we can believe now that is Everything that happens on earth has a reason behind it. The bell rang ' Ding Dong. Mandrid frequently ran and opened the door. Seeing his beloved, she got contented. Although emos was his adopted son but she took care of him and loved him a lot. Emos was the life of his parents and emos also loved his parents a lot but the secret with which the emos was not familiar was that he didn't know that he was the adopted son of the McQueen family. The McQueen family didn't thank that when emos will come to know that he was adopted, what will be his reaction and the consequences. Mandrid lifted emos in her hands and asked about his performance in the play. Emos answered that they were excellent during the play. The next day ,as usual emos was going to his school by his royal car suddenly he saw his friends and asked his driver to go with his friends on foot stubbornly. The driver asked his mother. As emos was stubborn at that time, his mother got agreed and was permitted to go to school with his friends. That time, he was going with Word, Sam, fam and one more guy whose name was Guy. The guy was one of the best friends of the emos. Why not? After all, Guy was the friend type material who correctly defined the statement " A friend in need is a friend indeed ". The group started their journey to school on foot. As the Word was the one who remained always jealous of the Emos, he planned a devilish plan for the Emos in his mind. In that mischief and as he told his plan to Sam and Fam, he got the support of Sam and Fam also as both were the best friends of Word. The mischief that was planned was that the emos was not familiar with all the roads to his school in Buckinghamshire Therefore emos was following the four where they were going. So, they planned that they will go to school through another path which was not familiar and known by the Emos in the morning with emos and guy and in the afternoon when they will go home from school on foot, they will challenge the emos to go back to school with the same path through which they came to school in the morning and as emos didn't know all the roads, he will be lost. Thinking that devilish plan, the word was feeling that his plan would end the partiality between them. As we all can understand very easily that the plan of Word was very harsh and devilish but at that time, he was only five years old and we know that a child of 5 years most probably every time wrong steps as he doesn't have a knowledge about that what is a crime? What is right decision or wrong decision ? The most important thing that if a person feels a partiality or a discrimination , his all time aim becomes to end that discrimination . In spite of ending partiality or removing discrimination , sometimes a person takes wrong steps which results in a crime . Word started his plan . When the group was walking pleasantly on the road suddenly Word asked that if they all wanted thrill and adventure in their pathway to school . In listening , his question was seeming a great idea for adventure . As the question ended , Emos was the one who raised his hand first . Seeing him , Guy also raised his hand . Emos was feeling very excited for their adventurous path but he didn't know that the adventure was a trap for him . Word told his friends to follow him for adventure. The Collingwood street ended . Then the St . Rollins Crossroad came . Word informed that to go school by the main road they had to take the left road and to go school by the adventurous path, they had to take the right road. The group took the right road and the adventure started. They walked for half an hour and reached school. They followed the Word but didn't find any adventure in their way. After getting annoyed, when emos asked Word when will be the adventure and thrill came? Word replied that Relax, it was just a prank. He smiled and ran towards the classroom. The prank spoiled the mood of the duo. When the duo entered class, the teacher punished them as they were late coming to school. Then the time came when the plan was about to end. The bell rang and all students came out of school. The driver was waiting at the gate to pick up the emos. Emos sat in his car and was ready to go suddenly Guy asked him if he will come with him as he came in the morning. Emos thank for a while and agreed to go with him on foot. That appeal was the Golden appeal that time for Word as the appeal saved his plan. Driver gone back to work. As the driver gone, Word frequently came and completed his plan . He challenged emos to go back home with the path with which they came in the morning. First, emos disagreed straightaway and said that he didn't believe in challenges. Listening to him, word started scolding him that he didn't have the guts to accept the challenge. After word's sledging, Emos got ready. Might be it was a wrong step by emos. Emos started his challenge with his bestie . Walking down to that unknown path, Guy asked whether Emos known the way or not . Emos replied that he had a road map in his mind when they were coming in morning, he made a map in his mind . Listening that , Guy got glad . When they were walking on Myra street , they saw the Sunshine crossroad . Guy asked " Where we have to go Emos ? " Emos took a look of that road and said that they had to take right . Guy asked " How are you show sure ? " Emos said that they had to take that path of sunshine crossroad on which a soldier stwas gone was building . Listening him , he would not able to stop him to appreciate Emos for his deep observing and his intelligence in a little age of 5 years old . He appreciated Emos with saying " Wow , you are a true observer " . Just like this , the duo walked further and further and in half an hour , both reached their houses . After that challenge , when the word saw the Emos walking happily, he got frustrated and confused that how the Emos completed that challenge . That moment , word ' s world was revolving around him and he was in a great depression and perplexity . When Emos reached home , his mother took a sigh of relief as she got very worried for Emos. Seeing him, his mother firstly scolded him and then asked Why he had been got late. Then, On behalf of Emos, Guy replied " Aunt, he is brilliant. He is a deep observer. Please don't scold him and instead of scolding him, please appreciate him, we came here with another path from the school which was not the most familiar to us. Listening to his reply, Mandrid got angrier and again started scolding him and said " Emos, from now, you will study in the boarding school. It will be safer and more protected for you. " Being a loyal child, he accepted his mother's saying . After that Emos gave a weird stare to Guy as he had ruined the situation . Then , Guy understood that if he hadn't said that much in front of Mandrid that time , Might be the Situation was some different . Although that school incident resulted in the admission of Emos to Boarding school but it also showed the first Glimpse of the Deep Observance of Emos.

6

EMOS MCQUEEN : THE COMING OF AGE

Into the boarding school, in the room quarter, on the floor bed, Guy was sleeping a pleasant sleep. Everything was okay till our hero didn't come. The bell rang. The guy was surfing on small tidal waves in the Pacific Ocean suddenly a big tidal wave came and the guy got drowned in that great tide. He was watching the dream and in the real life, the great tide was the bucket of water which was dropped by the emos to ruin the guy's dream. Frequently guy woke up and ran toward the bathroom. Then emos said, "Hey come out, you had already taken bath earlier in your dream ". When the guy noticed it, he said " Yeah, the great tide had already drowned me and Let we go to the science class, it is high time " The guy was a lazy one and he was the one who lived his life in his dream, because of this reason, Lovingly Emos called Guy as the Free Guy. It suits him better. As they both were already late for science class, both ran quickly to the classroom. Although emos was smart, intelligent and a vigilant one but he didn't like science so far. He wanted to become a businessman by taking commerce . When the duo was going to classroom suddenly emos got stopped and said that he didn't wanted to go to science class that day . Listening him , Guy got a patient of perplexity. He scolded him but it didn't affect emos so far . Emos told him to do his proxy. As Guy didn't had any other choice , at last he got ready . Guy entered in class with a smiling face but teacher didn't took a look of him and punished him straightaway . After a while , teacher called guy back in the class . Then the most worrying moment came for Guy . Teacher started taking attendance. The names were calling down, and the heartbeats of Guy were raising. The teacher called " Guy ". In reply, the guy replied " Yes Miss ". Then the time came in when Guy had two choices either he could be done proxy to save his friend or he could be told the teacher that Emos was missing to save the truth. At that time, Guy was not in a primary class, he was a senior one who studied in the 10th class with his friend. He could be taking the second choice but in spite of friendship, he chose the first choice. As the teacher called the Emos Name, Guy did his head down and did proxy for his friend. Let us find out what our upcoming protagonist was doing after bunking the class. The bell of the first period of that weekday rang. As the bell rang, frequently Guy ran to his quarters to find the Emos. He didn't found him for a long time. That day, Guy found emos behind the hostel where he was lying on the ground intoxicated. Seeing him, Guy got worried and frequently called his friends and Principal, Mr Stank. Mr Stank called an ambulance and emos got admitted to hospital. While treating him doctor got shocked. The doctor said that Emos had taken a large number of drugs during the last 5 hours.

Listening to his answer, the guy and stank got shocked and scared. The effects of the drug were also showing on the body of emos as it resulted in dark spots under the eyes of emos. Mr . Stank called the police to enquire about that horrible case. When Emos got waked up, he got scared as the cops were standing in the front of the emos eyes . In a harsh voice , the Inspector General of Cops , Mr. Sebestian started enquiry . He started his enquiry with asking that if emos had taken drugs or not . In a low voice , Emos said " No " . Really He was saying truth as he didn't known that what are drugs , what side-effects the drugs had ? Might be He got scared also . The main problem was that the officer didn't known the complete truth which was to be revealed soon. Sebestian got angry and gave a tight slap to him . Emos regurgitate each and every truth . He said that In afternoon , he bunked his Science class to met his some college friends who met him last day . Then Sebestian asked what was the reason of that meeting. Emos replied that when he met his college friends first time , they told him that they had a secret powder which could make a person more intelligent and smart and as he was a person who had a curiosity to be smarter than anyone. Therefore, he became a victim of his curiosity. Then, the next day when he bunked his school and met his college friends, they played a very devilish game with him and his life. They taught him to take the drugs and after that he got intoxicated and rest was the result. When all the people who were present there got scared, stupefied, stunned whatever you say but they were not in a state in which they could believe that our youth is going in right hands. From next day, the cops started their search for the guilty. It was the Sebestian Hard work or the god's blessing, we can't justify it. Sebestian found the Criminal group that supplied the drugs in only 2 days. He locked the devils in the prison. As he locked them suddenly their parents came and started arguing with them. They argued with Sebestian that if they had any evidence about their children . Sebastian bravely said that Evidences will be present in the Court trial . Before the devils were presented in trial , the families of the criminals together wiped out all the evidences with their power of wealth as they all were belonged to the rich section of society . As the system didn't had any evidence , therefore they had to left that devil criminals . It was not the first case in which police had to face such failure in attempting for Justice . This type of incident were common at that time . That incident made Emos very melancholic . It was nearly broken the heart of Emos . After that incident, although emos successfully recovered physically still he was enabled to recover mentally or we can say that he was mentally upset at that time. The time passed, and months changed, Emos passed his class 10th boards with a less percentage. Might be it was all the effect of that mental stress and that horrible incident. His marks were horror for him, his marks were as much as less that he had only one choice in the stream choosing which was the Arts Stream. As he wanted to be a scientist in his future from his childhood and when he got into the Arts stream, from then he started to be depressed and dissatisfied as his dream was killed by his own gaffe . One thing which was good with him after that incident was that he became a very good friend of the Inspector General of Cops , Mr. Sebestian . One day , as usual emos was reading the political science in library suddenly Mr. Sebestian came . Emos was not happy at that time . Actually ,he remained sad always after his boards . Seeing him , Mr . Sebestian laughed a little and asked what was his aim to be in his life and Congrats Now you are in the 11th class .

Keep studying my boy . Listening him , Emos started crying and said that he didn't wanted to talk with Sebestian . Motivating him ,Sebestian told him that he could share his problem with him with which he was annoyed and again asked about his future aim. Emos asked him if he will tell emos why those drug criminals were not punished. Sadly, Sebestian told him that If he told him shortly, the criminals were not punished because of the politics which was played with them during the case. Emos asked if Sebestian had any solution present for that bad politics. Sebestian said that he didn't have any solution for this politics but if our youth made an agenda in their mind to end the corruption and bad politics, so it will surely put an end to that type of crime one day. Listening to his answer, Emos got motivated and inspired . He said " Ok Mr Sebestian, I had chosen my aim". Sebestian frequently asked What it was. Emos answered, " Our nation needs more cops to end this corruption and to maintain an equality balance among them, therefore I am choosing my aim to be a fearless cop ". Listening to his answer, Sebestian got dissatisfied and said " Hey look at me, I am not a good or a fearless cop ". Emos got confused and replied " No, you are a good and fearless cop but why are you asking that ? Laughing a little, Sebestian said " Our nation has multiple numbers of talented cops as me but one person which our nation doesn't have still is an Honest, smart and intelligent advocates and lawyers. The Greedy, selfish advocates are a curse to our nation, whenever the people like them take bribes from anyone, that moment gives birth to corruption. So, my child, you are a deep observer, I had listened to it from your friend who's name is might be the free guy or whatever, It's my request if you want to serve yourself for your nation, Please be a Believer, trustworthy, truth revealing and an honest advocate. It will be best for you. It suits you, my son, It suits you. The last statement of Sebestian became the Golden statement for emos, it motivated him a lot and he intended to be that person who was needed by his nation. At last, he replied to Sebestian “ Yeah it suits me and motivating suits you ”. Then Sebestian smiled and went back to his department. That time was the turning point of Emos‘s life and as we know Our Serious Sebastian was the game-changer. From that day, Emos took an oath and passed his 12th board with a percentage of 99.7 % in Humanities. After all, he was influenced and inspired and all his marks were showing his hard work and his sacrifice. After school passed out, he enrolled himself in Oxford Brookes University when he was only 19 years. At that time, he was such a lean person in law that might be he had donated everything to his aim. He did the prestigious course MA LLB (MASTER OF ARTS). Then, after the 3 years, the time came when our protagonist became one of the most educated advocates of the United Kingdom. At a young but mature age of 23 years, he successfully became one of the most known and all-time great advocates of the United Kingdom. His dream was half fulfilled at that time but half was still left. That was truly the coming of age of Our one and only Emos McQueen where he became stand on his legs, became a self-employed, mature person and started thinking about the well being of his nation.

7

THE LIFE AS THE LAWYER

The Judge declared his judgement. The Guilty was taken for ensnarement. As the court adjourned, Emos started to pack his all things suddenly judge, Mr. Collingwood asked How emos did the interrogation much better than any other person. Emos smiled at him and said, " My lord, it's my secret or my hard work whatever you say but If I will reveal my technique for interrogation to everyone then what will be my requirement left ". His reply was as dashing as him. Might be that time, he was living a thug life. Therefore he was giving such thug replies to everyone. Emos came out, unlocked his bike, started it and went back to his house, Alfred. One day, Emos was reading his law books for enhancing his knowledge in the lawn of Alfred. He had his own 4 ways to be motivated and enthusiastic always which were the following :

1st: Know Your Worth
2nd: Sacrifice and Control Your emotions
3rd: Never Settle
4th: Keep Going

The above points were also the keys to his great success. When he was reading suddenly an old man came to him and started crying in front of him. Seeing him crying, emos also got emotional. Emos asked him if he wanted anything. The old man told his name as Macquire McQueen. Emos got amazed and said " Wonderful, I also belong to the McQueen family and my dad's name is also Macquire McQueen ". Macquire replied that He knew that. After that, he said that the name of his late son was also Emos McQueen. All it was the game of supreme being that the father and son were sitting in front of each other but didn't know their relation. Emos again asked him if he wanted anything. Macquire told him that he wanted to fill a case against a lady who had seized his land with false methods and malpractices. Then emos told Macquire that he wanted to know the total case from starting to end. Macquire explained to him that once 20 years ago, a mysterious fire broke out which resulted in the death of his son , death of his sister in law , death of his all cattle , his pet animal and burning of my farm . Listening his sorrow and grief , Emos started to think and asked Macquire if he had doubt on anyone that time . Macquire shakes his head with a disappointment . Emos relied him and gave him confidence that they will win . Then , Macquire continued his case, After that Mysterious fire , his farmland became unfertile. It resulted in a devastating famine in his family . One day, he met a man who looked like a forest officer. When Officer offered a very profitable offer , Mac wouldn't be abled to refuse that last choice in that famine situation. When Mac explained the offer it was that On the unfertile land of Macquire, the officer wanted to make a storehouse on the rent of 3300 dollars every month. As Mac accepted the offers, the officer handover him the first tariff and built a storehouse on that land. Five years later after that, Mac started to notice that on every 29th of every month, a truck came and left some 40 – 50 sacks every time the truck visited the storehouse and on every 18th of every month, again the truck came but that time they carried all the sacks which were present in the storehouse. That arrival of the truck on the constant dates made Macquire thank about that what things were stored in that storehouse. Then, Macquire thank a lot but didn't get any conclusive answer to his question. Therefore, he started ignoring it. He further explained the case that as the former farmland of Macquire was situated in the countryside of Buckinghamshire, therefore there was no registration system introduced earlier in that area and he didn't have any registry of his farmland in his name. The officer knew it much better. Might be he had planned the macquire worse earlier. When the registration system of land was introduced in his area 1 month ago, he didn't have any knowledge about it. Taking the advantage of Macquire unawareness, the officer frequently went to the registration system and registered the land under his name. Officially but dishonestly, the officer became successful in seizing Macquire's land. Emos McQueen understood the total case. Seeing him thinking about his case, Macquire got a hope that He can get his land back to him. Macquire asked if emos will litigate his case or not. First, Emos didn't say a single word but After some time he got ready and said that he will surely litigate his case and will try his best to give him justice. Macquire thanked him and asked if they had met earlier. Emos didn't answer anything and went to his cabin to file the Macquire McQueen Case. Then he remembered that he didn't have any phone number or address of Macquire so how will he enquire him for his case. Fortunately, Macquire was still standing in the lawn, why ? It can't be concluded . Emos asked macquire if he will come with him or he will give his phone number to talk . Macquire replied that It was his fortune that Emos was litigating his case . At last he said that he will done both the works . Macquire told his phone number as 07781 126456. Macquire told that the name of the lady who had seized his land was Harper James. After that, they both went to the Court and filed the case of Macquire against the Harper James. then they both went to the house of Macquire in the Bentley of Emos McQueen. With a pleasing car, a pleasing journey ended. Both reached the Macquire's grotty, old but his own house. Then, emos started studying the case and collecting the shreds of evidence. When the emos was seeing that storehouse suddenly he saw a lady in front of him. The lady was none other than who had seized the land of Emos, Harper James. She was expecting that because of his sudden appearance, emos will be frightened but nothing happened the same as she was thinking. Emos laughed a little and with a dashing smile he said " Oh, so you are the misery of Mr Macquire ". Frightening she asked who he was. He replied that He was Emos. Before he completed his name, Harper James asked if he was Emos McQueen. Emos replied," By chance but you have caught right ". Then James replied that She knew much him better than his parents from childhood . Listening him , Emos got choleric and asked who the hell she was . She replied " Whatever you say I am your heaven, I am your hell ". Listening to her all conversation, one more task was added to his cap to find that was How she knew him from his childhood. The conversation nearly distracted the emos from his case. At that time emos was not such busy as he remained busy in his other cases. His improper attention to the case made Macquire McQueen a little worried. Might be the case was already earlier solved by the emos in his mind. After almost a month, the date of the first trial came. Emos reached a little late in the court. Then Judge announced to start the case. Then the case started :

Harper James's Lawyer, Advocate Seron: My lord! The Macquire family are blaming us for seizing their land that is already registered under the name of my client

Judge : (to Advocate Seron) What proof do you have that the land is of your client?

Advocate Seron : (showing proof to the judge) Here it is my lord.

Judge : (Seeing the registration proof) Ya, it is ok Mr Seron. (Saying to the Emos McQueen) Do you want to say anything, Mr McQueen, by this proof, this case is seeming crystal clear.

Emos McQueen : (sitting on a chair in a straight manner and a good posture, he get up and started his argument) Ya, My lord I have much to say. First of all, I want to say that this land for which we are here doesn't belong to either my client or Harper James.

(Everyone got shocked even Macquire also got shocked but the one person who didn't get shocked was the Harper James)

Judge : (shockingly to the Emos) What are you saying? Have you lost your mind? See the registration proof document first before saying anything.

Emos McQueen: Keep patience, my lord, I will explain everything. (Giving the true documents of that land to judge) First, see the true documents of that land. (Judge got shocked)

Judge : (to the Emos) is it true?

Emos McQueen: Yes My lord the land for we are here is indeed government property. So how can anyone register it under his name?

Judge : (to the Advocate Seron) Now, tell Mr Seron. How do you register the land under the name of your client?

(As the Seron didn't have an answer, so Eros revealed it)

Emos McQueen : (Presenting the Head of Registration office, Mr Wilson) My lord he is the person who was bribed by the Harper James to make a duplicate registration proof of that governmental property.

Judge: Mr McQueen, I want to ask, how you caught Mr Wilson

Emos McQueen: My lord, I caught him with my unbeatable interrogation technique and my lord, I want one more favour from you, can you please arrange the amount of pension for my client monthly as he is an aged person so he can't do the work for a living and the only source of income for him was his land.

Judge: Sure, we must help the poor and arrange the pension for needed ones. So, I am declaring my judgement that is In the charge of misleading the government, in the charge of making fraud documents, Mrs . Harper James is sentenced for a 2 years prison and As the Mr Macquire is above the 60 years old, therefore the government is issuing his monthly pension of 2000 Dollars. The Court is adjourned.

At that moment, Emos was the WISEMAN for his real father. That day, Emos understood the Joy of giving to someone as he had helped Mr Macquire by giving him justice. Although emos didn't had known that Mr Macquire is his real father but he had helped his father indirectly. That incident properly defined that Everything is done by God whether it is good or bad. Although Emos was not successful in returning the land to his father, one thing that he did best was that he insured his father's living with that monthly pension. Three years later, Macquire McQueen (here I am talking about the stepfather o emos) received a notice for a summon in the court. In the notice, it was written that Mr McQueen supplied drugs and toxicity among the youth. Therefore he had called for a summon in the court. As he was a big industrialist, the notice made a huge loss in his industry shares and his reputation. When Emos came to know that His father had been called for a summon in the court, he got shocked and decided to litigate his dad's case. Seeing him so shocked and emotional about his dad, Mr McQueen advised him not to interrupt and interfere in his case and said that his competitors had planned a devilish trap for him. Whatever Macquire advised him , all got ignored by the Emos as he had decided to litigate his dad's case . One day emos was sitting in the garden and studying his father's case suddenly Word came to him and relied him that they will win . Emos smiled at him but he didn't know at that time that the person who gave him confidence will betray him. Then, the day of one of the biggest betray in the life of Emos came. The case started. The case took very less time than the last case to end. But that time the result came was not the same as the result of the last one. Emos lost the case. Before losing the case, that moment emos was winning the case suddenly the public prosecutor presented his Ace of Spades. His Ace of Spades was the Word. Yes, you have read right, Word, the friend who was giving confidence to emos sometimes earlier then came in court as a witness. Word witnessed that Macquire McQueen had once met him at a party and sold out several drugs by saying them energy powders to him. Word finished his statement and that moment also finished the chapter of the friendship between the two. That broke Emos's heart and witnessed one of the biggest betrayals in Emos's life. His witnessing in court was enough in court to declare that Macquire McQueen was a drug smuggler and a drug supplier. The Judge adjudged Macquire as a druggist and punished him with a Life imprisonment. Although Macquire had didn't supplied any drugs or whatever you say but sometimes everything is not happen as we wish . That day , that year went out a bad one for the Emos. That case became a headline in the English Times. Two years later, an English director came to our protagonist for an interview. His name was Paxton Lactose. Emos got ready for his first interview. In almost an hour Paxton took his total interview successfully. One of the most inspiring sayings of Emos during his interview was that He said " As we know life is a battleground where we all struggle and stand. It is a ground where we all see the ups and downs. It is a ground on which we all have a choice whether we want to be a coward or a brave. When I have to choose what I want to be, I chose to be a brave man. I choose to be a lawyer. From that point, I had seen both victories and defeats constantly on the battleground of life. One thing with which I will end my answer is that Being a Lawyer, you have to be strong and it is necessary to be confident while living a life as a lawyer. In short, Life as a Lawyer is not easy! That interview inspired Paxton a lot and he decided to make a movie on the life of Emos. He named his movie The Life as a Lawyer. His movie proved to be a blockbuster and became a golden jubilee in theatres. And why not the movie defined the life of emos as a lawyer!

Postscript Afterword

One day emos was watching the movie Mr. Cool in the theatre suddenly he started getting the fits. As the public was busy watching Mr. Cool, no one noticed him. After almost 10 minutes, he got normal. The movie ended in an hour. The audience started leaving the theatre. As everyone was leaving, emos also decided to leave. When he was coming downstairs suddenly he collided with an aged man. Seeing emos, the man got relentless, impatient, and shocked ....

9 798887 046389

Printed by Libri Plureos GmbH in Hamburg,
Germany